One 'n Done #6

THE PATH HOME

A novella by
AJ Pellegrino

Published by

Published by Read Furiously - Trenton, NJ. First Edition.

ISBN: 979-8-9868097-8-6
Library of Congress Control Number: 2022949692

Short Fiction
Romance
LGTBQIA+

This is a work of fiction. Names, characters, business, events and incidents are the products of the author's imagination. Any resemblance to actual persons, living or dead, or actual events is purely coincidental.

For more information on *The Path Home* or Read Furiously, please visit readfuriously.com. For inquiries, please contact info@readfuriously.com.

Read Often. Read Well.

Read Furiously

PART I

"Bryn, come on!" Iris's command was a harsh whisper as both girls sprinted fearlessly through the woods. They were far from the path, with only the bobbing lights from their phones to illuminate the way.

"You're going too fast! Iris!" came Bryony's huffed reply, her feet crunching through the thick green vegetation that coated the forest floor.

Their town's annual bonfire night, to usher in the beginning of summer, was the most elaborate either of them had ever seen. Multiple barbecues were lit and the smell of grilled meat mingled with the freshly cut grass of the field before the large forest that surrounded their town. Elaborately decorated tables were piled high with baked goods and sparklers and cooler after cooler was packed with ice and sweating cans.

Long before the sun dipped behind the forest's tallest leaves, Iris and Bryony had plopped down in the grass along with three of their friends. They passed around the plastic water bottle filled with vodka to spike their drinks, talking and laughing until the muted sky gave way to fireflies around them.

Bryony's head was in Iris' lap as she unconsciously played with the hole at the knee in Iris' tights. She was only half listening to their friend Sean as he recounted a story at his older brother's expense. Iris had spent the afternoon braiding a plaited crown into Bryony's hair and, once she was satisfied, had started picking the white clover around them to adorn her work.

The clovers that managed to stay tucked in Bryony's hair were shriveled now, wilted from the heat but still a vibrant green. The rest fell from the loosening strands of Bryony's hair, leaving a trail of flowers in her wake. Both girls slowed down as the sticky late June air sat heavy in their greedy lungs. Both sets of eyes wide as they directed their lights frantically through the trees they knew would lead to the reservoir just beyond one of the hidden glades the teenagers liked to sneak off to on weekends.

"Did we lose the path?" Bryony was clutching at her side and shuffling about, trying to keep her balance. It created a harsh crunching throughout the otherwise quiet trees that surrounded them.

"Shh," Iris instructed, smashing an unsteady finger to her lips, that matched her glassy eyes. "No, it's this way."

Iris grabbed Bryony's hand and determinedly stomped west, and even though Bryony didn't necessarily trust Iris' tipsy sense of direction, she did not object. Instead she laced their fingers together and quickened her steps to keep up with Iris' shorter but more muscular legs. Bryony had been following Iris since they were little and she had no intention of stopping now.

"Do you think they're going to do it?" Iris asked when they finally reached a more level ground.

Bryony was thankful, now that the liquid in her stomach could stop sloshing back and forth. They really should have eaten more food. Earlier in the day, their group heard a couple of kids home from college talking about going skinny dipping in the town's reservoir. Iris had smirked down at Bryony with a mischievous look in her eye, a look Bryony knew all too well.

"Of course they are," Bryony snorted. She suddenly felt winded and looked up into the sky above her to try and catch her breath. "They've definitely done it before." She spoke the words to the tops of the trees and the moon above instead of to Iris.

As if she was jealous, Iris stuffed her phone in her back pocket and took Bryony's face in her hands. She dipped the taller girl's face to look at her. "And how would you know that?"

Bryony wanted to smirk down at her, but Iris' fingers were so close to her mouth now and all Bryony wanted was to feel them drag across her bottom lip. She wanted a repeat of the weekend before in Amy's basement when they'd played spin the bottle and Iris had placed a chaste kiss on her lips.

They'd been dancing around it for years, and still the dance would go on because Bryony didn't want to push. Iris was always so much better at taking the lead.

"Wouldn't you like to know," she finally managed with a teasing air.

It came out in gusts of vodka and knock off soda that lingered between them before they both broke into strained giggles. It swelled between them until both girls clung to each other in the heat, not caring that their skin stuck together or that sweat was pooling in their creased angles.

In the beam of light from Iris' phone, the shadows of the underbrush rippled with life behind them. The thick leaves bristled and straightened, then leaned towards both girls as if they were casting rays of light that the foliage could absorb. Through the edges of the dusty, dirt path, new blades of grass began poking up. It blurred the borders of the path and the dense ivy leaves that shuffled together in the outskirts of their vision. Neither girl noticed, too preoccupied with the other's cheek pressed to their own to care about anything else.

"Quietly," Bryony whispered while their chests heaved as their laughter died down.

Iris nodded, still shaking with silent giggles and wiped a tear from her eye. Then, without warning, she took off, running as fast as her soccer toned legs would carry her.

"Hey!" Bryony yelled and took chase.

"Quietly!" Iris' sing-song voice called back in the dark, only her forgotten phone illuminating the path behind her. "Shit!"

The light went dead for a second as the phone slipped out of her back pocket to kiss the ground. It gave Bryony the time she needed to catch up as she took off past Iris, now confident she knew which direction to turn for the glade before the reservoir. Her flashlight was making her dizzy as Iris' thunderous footfalls were gaining on her.

"Gotcha," Iris hissing in her ear as she barreled into Bryony and sent them hurtling towards the earth. They both shrieked in laughter and jumped to their feet again, brushing dirt and bits of blood from their knees.

"This way," Bryony said and even though she was leading, Iris was still the one in front.

Her fingers were hooked in Bryony's belt loop, like she couldn't be any further from her. Like she needed to know Bryony was there with her and hadn't disappeared into the darkness. As they approached the glade, Iris tugged hard and sent Bryony hurtling after her into the nearest tree.

"Ow! What the - " Bryony started but Iris cut her off.

"Shh!" She fumbled with her phone until she finally got her flashlight to turn off. "Turn it off, turn it off." Bryony fumbled with her own phone until her beam of light was also extinguished as demanded.

The darkness settled in around them. It pressed

in, embracing them in the heat that rose to their heads as their adrenaline pumped in their veins. Only the fireflies provided any source of immediate glow. One was so close to Iris' hair that Bryony wanted to reach out and catch it and present it to her as a gift. It was a childish desire awakened from when the two of them would play hunter in Iris' backyard. As dusk fell they'd present their prizes to each other, pressed close together, foreheads touching, to keep their own fireflies from escaping. The flickering light from their cupped hands would illuminate the wonder in Iris' dark eyes and the dimples of Bryony's smile.

A loud whooping made both of them jump. Their eyes were beginning to adjust to the dark and in the distance, across the glade Bryony could see two shapes. Iris grasped at Bryony's wrist as she moved closer to the trees that lined the small open grass.

Whoever was a few yards from them wasn't the source of the noise. A loud splash sounded a few seconds after the cry and Iris sighed in relief against Bryony's back where she'd pressed herself. The reservoir was just beyond the far trees.

"Who is that over there?" Bryony whispered, painfully aware of how quiet the forest was around them. Even the chirping and buzzing and rustling couldn't mask the volume of their voices.

She leaned against the nearest tree and let out a huff. Iris didn't leave her space, but gave Bryony enough room to lean her back against the tree instead. She was so close, and then she took a step closer.

"They'll see," Bryony whispered when Iris's lips were ghosted over her own. Her skin was on fire and she was so acutely aware of the taste of alcohol still on her tongue.

"I don't care," Iris said. Her hands rested on Bryony's hips as if she wasn't sure where else to put them. "As long as you don't care."

"I don't care," Bryony said quickly.

That was all the confirmation Iris needed before crashing her lips against Bryony's. It was desperate and sloppy and made Bryony's head spin. She pulled Iris close and she squeaked in surprise before kissing Bryony harder.

All around them there was a soft rustling again. The flowers that had closed hours ago began to open in full bloom. Small patches of green moss that coated smatterings of tree trunks began to spread, sprouting small mushrooms in its wake. Slowly, ivy began to snake its way towards their feet.

Before the two of them could break apart for air, a deadpanned "get a room" was called to them from across the glade. The girls jolted apart but didn't let go of each other. They smiled at each other, but Iris sunk into a frown.

"What is it?" Bryony asked, her mind jumping to a million different things she must have done wrong.

"Your flowers are gone," Iris pouted. She lifted her hand to pat at the now loose braids in Bryony's hair.

Bryony rolled her eyes and laughed. Iris took both of her hands and pulled her from the tree trunk. They both made their way slowly back to the bonfire, hand in hand, kissing or giggling the entire walk back.

*

The forest watched them go. The forest felt them leave.

PART II

"Mom?" Bryony's voice rang out cool and crisp through the house.

It echoed the returning leaves and heady air after winter's lingering chill had ebbed away. It sounded like her favorite season. But it didn't quite feel like her favorite season, not yet. Spring was sticking around as stubbornly as the snow had through March. The city sidewalks had stayed slushy and gray until early May.

"Mom?" Bryony called again, dropping the two garbage bags of clothes by the front door. She let the door swing shut behind her, but the wood had already started to swell. She needed to slam it before swinging a backpack off and venturing further in.

Being home was like entering an entirely different season. The early June humidity helped, but it was that nostalgic feeling, that longing for summer nights at the reservoir or in the woods that pulled her back to a heat that was not quite there yet.

"Oh, mother?" She tried in a sing-song tone,

side-stepping that one warped spot of the living room floor. A sure sign the heat was well on its way.

The house was exactly as she had left it a little over two years ago to start a summer job before her junior year. Bryony felt a pang of guilt in her chest that she had kept finding reasons not to take the four and half hour drive home sooner.

The house was small and rustic, for sure in need of an update or two, but was adorned with original accents and filled to the brim with handcrafted furniture. The rocking chair closest to the door was still piled high with all of the half finished scarves and hats that her mom had started in the fall when she decided to pick up crocheting. She recognized them from their video chats.

Usually around this time the house was still closed up against the cold, but Bryony saw that her mom had the windows thrown open and every fan on the first floor was on. She thought it was a bit premature and wrapped her thin sweatshirt around her shoulders a bit more snuggly. Her mother was still nowhere to be found.

"Mom?" Bryony tried again, a slight worried edge to her voice now.

"Well look at you," her mom's voice boomed from behind her as the older woman shoved her way through the front door. "Not even back five minutes and you've begun taking over the house!"

Bryony wheeled around and stared at her mother with a smile spreading onto her face. Her mother was only slightly taller than she was, with softer curves than she'd had while Bryony was growing up, smile lines for days, and a shock of gray hair tied up in a messy bun on top of her head. Her mother was turning sixty-two in a few months' time and if Bryony looked like her mother at that age, she would thank all of her foremothers for her good genes.

"Well?" Her mother asked, her hands on her hips. "Are you just going to stand there and stare at me?"

Bryony realized that she hadn't actually moved to hug her mom yet, too caught up in seeing her for the first time since graduation two weeks ago. They hadn't had too much time together after the ceremony, just a quick celebration dinner before her mom drove back upstate. She took a few long strides forward and wrapped her mom in a tight hug.

"Missed you," Bryony said into the soft sweater covering her mom's shoulder.

"Missed you too, Bryn," Dawn said, her cheek pressed against the top of her daughter's copper toned head.

They stayed like that for a minute before breaking apart. Bryony stepped back and Dawn took a long hard look at her.

"What?" Bryony asked, a familiar sense of unease settling in under her mom's scrutinizing gaze.

"You haven't been eating," her mom said. "I saw you two weeks ago and somehow you look thinner."

"The city is expensive, mom," Bryony bristled. Especially when you no longer have a meal plan to fall back on, but she kept that bit to herself. She didn't want her mom's scrutinizing to turn to agitation. She bent down to grab the two garbage bags and hauled one over her shoulder.

"Is that why you're home?" She asked, grabbing Bryony's discarded backpack.

Bryony froze. She hadn't considered the idea that she might not be welcome home and now the thought that being gone for so long had been a mistake.

"Not that I don't want you back!" Dawn said quickly, almost like she could read the thoughts racing through Bryony's mind. "I just thought you had that fellowship lined up for the summer in Brooklyn."

"I did," Bryony threw over her shoulder as she started up the stairs to her bedroom. The old wood protested under her weight with each step. She mulled over that thought as she opened the first door on the right. At least her mom hadn't turned the small room into a storage space. "It's just…well, the city is expensive."

Bryony didn't know how to verbalize that she had started feeling drawn back to this place the closer graduation drew near. She knew what it would sound like if she told the truth; that every decision she made about her future that didn't include being in this town felt wrong. The campus GP had given her a referral to the campus therapist when she tried to explain it. She had said it was probably generalized anxiety centered around breaking away from her sense of comfort after graduation. Bryony hadn't known how to break it to her that she'd spent a while avoiding her town, along with one person in particular.

"You know I could have helped, sweetheart," Dawn said.

Bryony didn't want to turn to look at her, but she could see her mom's slightly warped face in the window in front of her. She knew her mom couldn't have afforded that, but that wasn't why she pulled out.

"I've actually been looking into fellowships around here," Bryony lied. She turned now to smile at her mom in a way she hoped was convincing.

"Oh," Dawn said. She tried to quickly turn her look of surprise into one of encouragement. "That's great, I didn't realize you could still apply for summer fellowships."

"Not summer ones, no," Bryony winced. "I'm applying for the fall and I figured I could get a job in the meantime."

Dawn fiddled with the top strap of Bryony's backpack. She clearly wanted to say something.

"What?" Bryony sighed. She had known this would be coming, it was inevitable. She just didn't want to do this now.

"It's just…you went to art school, you were living in the city, and you seemed to like it. This place is…" Dawn struggled for words.

"Rural?" Bryony helped.

"Out of the way." Dawn finished. Bryony couldn't help but chuckle. She started to walk back towards her mom to get the rest of her things from her car but her mother took her arm to stop her. She rubbed up and down Bryony's arms the same way she used to when Bryony would get startled by the loud crack of a late night thunderstorm. "I just want to make sure you're making the right decision here."

"I am." Bryony said with an air of finality. "I'm just, I don't know, drawn to this place. I've always been drawn to this place." It was the best way she could describe that feeling twisting in her chest. "And besides, if I can't afford it here, how am I supposed to afford anywhere in the city?"

"Drawn here, huh?" Dawn asked and Bryony nodded in answer. "Alright, well, then I have a graduation gift for you."

Bryony hadn't expected a graduation gift. She assumed getting to live at home rent free for a bit was the gift. She followed along behind her mom as she led her down the stairs and back through the living room, out the front door, across the driveway, through the gardens and towards the two door garage. It stood about ten feet away from the side of the house that had the chimney attached to it and never had a car residing in this garage as long as Bryony had lived there. Which was her whole life.

"Tada!" Dawn said as she opened the garage doors.

Bryony looked around expecting there to be something different about the large space, but there was nothing. The forgotten or old garden tools that her mother had no use for would wind up in here over the years. Broken pots, dried out bulbs, and forgotten books were piled high and littered the corners at almost every turn. The only real use this place had had since Dawn had bought it was storing the firewood they needed for the winter. The last of the logs from that season were still stacked by the door.

"Uh," Bryony began, trying to hide her questioning voice. Her eyes, which swept over the garage quizzically, however, gave her away. "Thank you?"

Dawn was leaning against the wall watching as her daughter tried to find the gift. She giggled before walking in after her.

"Well, see, I think that your silk screening equipment can go here." She turned Bryony to face the corner of the garage that got the least amount of sun; currently it was occupied with rusted hoes and rakes. "And here," Dawn turned Bryony again towards the two large windows facing out towards the woods, "is where I figured your painting and sketches could go. There's enough room for your easels and with a table put in you could hold all of your supplies." By this point, Bryony was fighting an emotion she hadn't expected from breaking out of her chest. "And here," her mother walked her right into the middle of the space, "is where you can set up your sculptures."

"It's gonna need some heat." Bryony's voice held a thickness that betrayed the overwhelmed feeling in her chest.

"Yeah," Dawn agreed. "I figure a futon or blow up mattress too. If you keep up that college work schedule of yours."

"Hey!" Bryony protested, putting on a mock hurt voice. "Some of my best work is done between two to four o'clock in the morning."

"I know, sweetheart," Dawn draped her arm around her daughter's shoulders. "That's what I'm worried about." They stood there in vaguely comfortable silence as the heat from the midday sun began to settle in around them.

"Maybe an AC unit too." Bryony said. She realized that her mom had been right to have all those windows open inside.

"I guess you were right about that job," Dawn said and patted Bryony's arm before turning to stride back to the house.

Bryony snorted after her mom's retreating back before turning to survey the garage. She tried to envision how she would make her studio look. She would fill the space with herself. She would create things to be proud of. She would make sure she didn't make a mistake coming home.

"Here's hoping," she muttered and watched a daddy long legs scuttle across the hard floor. She cringed before shuffling out as well.

Bryony was halfway back to her car to start unloading the rest of her things when she noticed the sad state of the garden. It was, well, odd to see so many wilted greens and shriveling baby vegetables. Her mom had always had a green thumb, and while it was too early in the season for any vegetation to have made any large amounts of growth, it was certainly too early for the kind of decay that had settled in.

"That's weird," Bryony mused to herself as she crouched down to inspect the pitiful looking tomato plants.

Her fingertips brushed the coarse leaves gently as if she was afraid she might do further damage. She frowned before looking out over the rows of plowed dirt. She didn't see any hint of disturbance from animals or bugs either. There were no violent gaps where leaves had been chewed or disturbed piles of earth to show something had been digging.

Bryony stood straight again and trudged back off towards the car. Her thick boots contrasted with her pale green leggings that matched her sweatshirt. She blended in with the property around her and the woods not so far off in the distance. She'd always liked being able to fade away, it made her feel more at ease here.

"Bryn!" Her mom's voice floated through one of the open windows. "How much more stuff do you need to bring in? Should I start warming up the chili?"

⁂

"So, Mom," Bryony started. She might as well rip the band-aid off quickly.

They were both seated at the small round table they'd conversed and ate at all of Bryony's life. It was always a place of acceptance where Bryony could tell her mom just about anything. It seemed like it had just enough room for the two of them now. There was a distance between them, born of Bryony's college independence; short phone calls and missed holidays.

"I heard that Iris came back last summer." She tried to sound casual as she asked, but could hear that she was falling short. "How has she, I mean, have you seen her around at all?"

Bryony was so concerned with trying to make her hand not shake around the spoon she held that she missed the way her mom sucked in a breath and held it. Dawn's eyes lingered on the third chair at the table, the one Iris had occupied for so many meals when both girls were small.

"Uh, no, unfortunately," she started as she dipped her spoon into her bowl and moved her food around a bit. "Iris is, well, she's been keeping herself busy since she graduated and moved back into the area."

"Oh," Bryony said. She wasn't able to hide the disappointment in her voice. "Okay. So she's not still living with her dad?"

"No," her mom answered simply.

Bryony pushed her own food around with her

spoon and let the silence settle in around them. The ticking of the ceiling fan filled the room as Bryony took a mouthful of chili. She needed something to fill in the time it would take to think of something to say next.

"I was thinking of going into town tomorrow to visit Mona," Bryony said. "I haven't seen her and Nora since their wedding."

"That's a good idea," her mom says around her own mouthful. "I think their bakery is looking for a hostess."

"Sure, yeah, that might be nice."

It didn't take Bryony long to get all of her belongings from the living room, where she had dropped them, into her bedroom. She closed the door with an unintentionally loud thud and dropped down onto her bed, laying back on the soft comforter. It had a stale smell to it from so many months of neglect.

She pulled her phone out of her pocket. Three text notifications that she was ignoring from her best friend and no-longer roommate, Amelia, and one missed call from her mom from earlier. She opened

Instagram and scrolled mindlessly until she got up the nerve to search for Iris' profile in her list of followers.

She hadn't posted any pictures or stories in over a year, not since her own graduation. Not that it mattered. Iris had assured Bryony that neither states or the three hour time difference would come between them, but somewhere in Bryony's bones she had known that wasn't true. That summer had been laced with a melancholy that Bryony hadn't been able to shake, no matter how many times Iris tried to kiss it away.

When Bryony went off to school the next summer, she conceded to an understanding of why Iris had drifted away. It didn't erase the fact that it hurt, but she understood. They had been reduced to social media likes and comments; promises of catching up when they both went home for breaks. Neither of them ever came home.

Bryony had dated her fair share of girls in college. She hadn't let the emptiness that Iris left in her stop her from trying to move forward. She still let herself scroll endlessly through Iris' Instagram and watched every one of her Stories on nights when she felt loneliness consume her.

Tonight Bryony chewed on the nail of her thumb and slowly scrolled through the pictures she'd seen dozens of times already. If Iris had been home this whole year, or at least in the area, why had she gone completely MIA on all social media? Bryony thought Iris would have posted stories about how boring it was to be home, or, and Bryony's pulse sped up at this thought, would have DMed her with an embarrassing anecdote or two before her own return.

Wishful thinking, she realized before closing the app and placing her phone on her chest.

✳

A steady knocking on Bryony's bedroom door woke her. She groaned and looked at her phone screen. 7:45 am.

"Bryn," her mom's voice came through the gaps in the doorframe. "Bryn, I'm heading to work!"

"M'kay," Bryony said, pulling her comforter back up to her shoulders. Her ceiling fan was swinging lazily above her and now that Bryony was somewhat awake she couldn't ignore its squeaking.

"Bryn!" Her mom's voice is sharper now. "Don't

stay in bed all day!"

"M'kay," Bryony said louder now so her mom would stop her persistent knocking. "I'm getting up."

"Okay, I'll be home around four!"

"M'kay," Bryony mumbled into her pillow as retreating footsteps and creaking stairs indicated her mom's departure. She jumped slightly when the closing of the front door echoed through the quiet house.

Bryony tried to go back to sleep, but the squeaking of the fan kept pulling her back to consciousness. She groaned and dragged herself out of bed to slap the switch off. She threw herself back in bed and shoved her face into the pillow against the morning sun. She had almost drifted off to sleep again when her phone started vibrating.

"Yeah, Mom," Bryony sighed, agitation hard to keep at bay.

"I forgot to tell you," her mom's voice crackled through the car's bluetooth. "If you're going to be cleaning out the garage today, make sure to pile anything in good shape to donate." Bryony hadn't planned on cleaning out the garage today, but apparently that decision had been made for her.

"Bryn, can you hear me?"

"Yup. Clean out the garage," she said, rolling over and rubbing her face. "Keep anything in good shape to donate."

"Alright sweetheart," she said and Bryony heard her turn signal clicking in the background. "Well, don't waste the day. Love you!"

"I won't," Bryony said. "Love you too."

Bryony tried, once again, to go back to sleep, but her mind had woken up too much. She grabbed her phone again and started to scroll through her Instagram feed. She stopped on a picture of the apartment she was supposed to be moving into, its living room piled with half of everything that had been in their college apartment. She liked it and closed the app. As if she had her notifications turned on, which she probably did, a text from Amelia lit up on her screen.

Amelia

Bryony hated the weather this time of year. The mornings were cool and the days were warm. It made the bedrooms a sauna, the old radiator pipes trying to blast as much heat in as possible, and the rest of the house an icebox.

Bryony meandered downstairs and let her feet carry her to the kitchen. She fumbled around until she found the cabinet where her mom had stored her electric kettle and plugged it in. She found the half empty bag of her favorite coffee powder shoved into the pantry, untied the rubber band around it, and poured it into the largest mug she could find.

She could probably get half of the garage cleaned out by noon, she thought as she watched the water in the glass kettle begin to bubble. There wasn't a lot of junk in there, and that gave her more than enough time to shower and grab lunch at Mona's bakery before her mom got home. Hopefully, her mom would get off her case and let her sleep in once that task was done.

The kettle's shrill whistle brought Bryony out of her daze. She poured the steaming water into her mug and stirred before hunting down the milk. It wasn't that she wanted to lay around all summer, but she didn't have it in her to begin the application process for the fall just yet. Bryony had been excited to start her fellowship a few weeks ago, now nothing seemed less appealing than being away from this town.

She sipped her coffee slowly, walking to the kitchen window to look out over the dying garden. She didn't want to think about why she wasn't there, because she didn't have any answers, not even for herself. Surely sleeping until noon and watching reruns of *Bob's Burgers* for a few days would help her not think; at least for a little bit.

An hour later Bryony was dressed and trudging out the front door, empty coffee cup forgotten on her dresser. She had an ancient bluetooth speaker in hand that she'd dug out of the hallway closet, her own having been ruined a few months back in her senior studio, and was trying to get it to connect to her phone. The sun was high enough now that its warmth was enough to chase away any early morning chill. Bryony stopped dead when the speaker made a defeated noise once again and her phone declared it could not find the source to connect.

"Oh, come the fuck on," she muttered, holding the button down to try and sync the devices. She groaned loudly when it, once again, would not sync. "Fucking useless," she sighed, letting both hands that held each device drop to her sides.

She looked absently to her left, where her mom's garden was and was about to turn to go back into the house when a bit of green caught her eye. Under any normal circumstance it would have been completely normal to see the bright green of the tomato plant's leaves. Its stem straight and hearty, with little green tomatoes beginning to bloom on their vines. Except, that very same tomato plant had been shriveled and pathetic looking only yesterday and all the other plants around it still looked that way.

Bryony hummed to herself, a frown on her face as she stared at the offending fruit, that shouldn't have been offensive at all. She walked to her car and deposited her phone and the speaker on the hood then walked back up to the garden. Her eyes hadn't been playing a trick on her. That lone tomato plant was looking tiny, sure, but healthy.

She gently inspected its leaves, the stem, the tiny tomatoes, and nothing seemed odd about them. Then she turned her attention to the plant next to it and inspected it as well, brushing a finger on the leaves as gingerly as possible so as not to break them off. She turned to the beginnings of the squash in the row next to it and did the same. It wasn't like her mom to neglect the garden, but she could help out now.

Bryony walked around the paneled dirt towards the side of the house and unhooked the hose.

"Where's the - " she started before finding the nozzle under the second ring of hose. "Ah," she said and screwed it on before turning on the water.

She walked around the two patches of dying vegetation, making sure to cover every patch of dirt and every dying leaf with a light misting of water. It couldn't hurt. Maybe trying to bring everything back to life could be her destress project while she was home. She glanced towards the garage, it definitely wouldn't be setting up her studio.

She had to make the effort, though, so she grabbed her phone from the hood of her car, fished her headphones out of the center console, and set her path to the garage. She put on her gym playlist, which got very little use since she could never actually make herself go to the gym, and set to work. Maybe she could even get it all cleared out today.

Within an hour she was covered in dirt and didn't feel like she'd accomplished much. She pushed on, the pile of "to donate" tools growing much slower than the pile of garbage. The next time she looked at her phone it was two in the afternoon.

"Shit," she sighed. The beginnings of a headache were coming on from the heat and dehydration. There was no way she'd make it into town today so Bryony pushed on for another half an hour before her body began to protest her efforts.

Bryony stood in front of the open fridge for a while eating some cold cuts from the packaging before forcing herself to take a shower. The ache in her arms and legs was a clear indicator that, though she had been walking all over Manhattan the past four years, she wasn't in any kind of shape. The lukewarm water soothed her muscles as she slowly cleaned herself, groaning in pain when the bottoms of her feet protested with every shift of her weight.

She crawled into bed for a quick nap before her

mom got home. Her car door slamming registered somewhere in the back of her consciousness after what felt like days, but she was so tired she couldn't bring herself to stir. It wasn't for some time before Bryony heard a soft knock on her bedroom door.

"Bryn," Dawn said, quietly.

If Bryony could have brought herself to answer, she might have but sleep had tugged at eyelids again. The door closed a few seconds later.

Bryony was a teenager again. She couldn't see herself to confirm it, but she could feel it, she just knew. She was sixteen and walking out of her front door. Someone was ahead of her, walking towards the driveway, towards the garden, past the flimsy fence she used to jump, and towards the treeline of the forest.

She followed. There was no other logical path to take but the one the person in front of her was taking. Bryony knew this in her bones. She needed to follow this person, whose form seemed so familiar. And yet…

Bryony looked down, she wasn't sure why but she did, and saw dead grass under her feet. The path they were on was paved with dry, yellow grass that crunched under her bare feet. Now that Bryony was aware of it, she felt the sharp points of the blade breaking against her soft soles.

It hurt. Not in her feet, not against her skin, but in her soul. The dead earth that beckoned her towards the trees was crying out to her. She felt its pain. It brought tears to her eyes and she stopped next to the person she'd been following, right at the mouth of the forest. She wanted to help.

"Good," the person said in a voice that she knew. She knew it better than anything. She would follow it anywhere.

Bryony took a deep breath and blinked. The chill of the morning air settled in around her. The grass under her feet was dry, but not as dead as in her dream. The aching in her muscles, in her feet, settled back in. She turned quickly from the trees and looked around the clearing next to her house. There was no one else standing with her.

Bryony hugged her arms to her chest. She had fallen asleep in shorts and a tank top, which was not weather appropriate now that the sun was only just starting to rise over the tops of the trees. A panic sparked to life in her chest. She hadn't sleepwalked since her senior year of high school, and she had never left the house before.

Without looking back into the darkness of the trees, Bryony sprinted across the clearing towards the house. She eased the unlocked front door open quietly and sat down on the couch. She grabbed an end pillow and hugged it to her chest. Maybe she should call the campus therapist. Could she still call the campus therapist? Did she need to find a real life therapist? She definitely couldn't afford that.

The low growl of her stomach reminded Bryony that she had fallen asleep without eating anything but rogue cold cuts the day before. She walked to the kitchen with the pillow still clutched to her. There was a note from her mom on the fridge.

Leftovers in the fridge in case you
get some inspiration at 4am. XO

Bryony opened the fridge to see a tupperware container filled with spaghetti and meatballs. She contemplated the ramifications of eating dinner at - she looked at the stove's clock - 4am on the dot.

Another painful growl convinced her that they would be minimal.

It was six thirty when Dawn came down the stairs to the smell of coffee and red sauce. Bryony had never gone back to bed, instead she grabbed her laptop and paced the dining room with a thumbnail wedged between her teeth until she finally collapsed in a chair at the table. Since then she had been trying to log into her and her mom's insurance to see what mental health benefits they had. So far, she could find none.

"Morning, kiddo," her mom said with far too much pep for the hour. She squeezed Bryony's shoulder as she made her way to the kitchen. "I'm going to the store today, do you want me to pick up more of that coffee you like?"

"Huh?" Bryony asked. She already had a finished cup of coffee next to her screen. "Oh, yeah, that would be great," she said as her mom poured herself a bowl of cereal. "Thanks, mom."

"What are you doing up so early?" She took a seat next to Bryony after pouring her milk.

"Uh, fellowship research for the fall," Bryony said. She closed out the tab she was on. Thankfully she had a dozen others to switch to. "Oh, mom, I forgot to ask the other day." Her mom hummed her acknowledgement around a mouthful of cereal. "What's with your garden? Why is everything so dead?"

Dawn took her time chewing before she answered.

"We've had a real problem with pesticides the past few years," she said, finally.

"But you don't use anything with pesticides," Bryony countered.

"I know," Dawn said, taking another mouthful. "But that big farm a few miles up, the one that supplies the crops to the farmer's market. They changed everything over to organic to appease the no GMOs crowd and since then the pesticide runoff has been devastating."

Bryony didn't know enough about how organic vegetables were farmed at a commercial level to question her mom, but that didn't seem right.

"Is anyone else around here having that issue?"

"Oh yeah," her mom said. "Loads of people. All the gardens around here are being impacted by it. But I have a bone to pick with you, young lady," she said before Bryony could continue her line of questioning.

"What?" Bryony asked, not sure what she could have done before 7am to merit a stern talking to.

"You left my speaker outside on the hood of your car."

"Oh, sh - sorry, mom," she said, remembering that she had forgotten it outside.

"Just be more careful with other people's things," her mom said, then rose to put her empty bowl in the sink. Bryony frowned at her back. "So what are your plans for today? I saw you got a lot done in the garage yesterday."

"Yeah, but I think I need a break." Bryony stretched her arms above her head, despite the soreness in them. "My muscles hurt so bad. I'm thinking of heading over to Mona's bakery today since I didn't make it yesterday."

"Alright," Dawn gave her daughter a kiss on the top of her head. "Well, try and stay awake long enough to have dinner with me tonight, huh?"

"I'll try," Bryony chuckled.

A few Google searches about farm pesticides and another cup of coffee later, Bryony decided that it was an appropriate hour to make her way into town. She could walk. It would be about a half an hour walk, one she did all the time before moving to the city. One she could easily do now, she reasoned.

Halfway through her walk, Bryony realized driving would have been the smarter choice. Her feet were screaming, but she just walked faster. By the time she got to the Flour Power Bakery she had stopped multiple times to quickly chat with neighbors she'd known most of her life.

It felt…odd to be home, because it didn't feel like home anymore. Everything was the same. The same stores were there, maybe some updates here and there were done. The same cracks in the asphalt. The same stands on the sidewalk.

There was something different at the corners of this quaint picture. A feeling that Bryony couldn't quite put her finger on. It was like she didn't belong here anymore, like she didn't know where she belonged.

She let her mind wander back to her dream. She'd felt that same pull that she had for weeks. It had crept up her spine and tugged her towards the woods tugged her towards…

"Bryn!" Mona's voice pulled Bryony out of her thoughts.

Her feet had carried her straight into the bakery.

The front had a few empty tables that looked out on the main street. The front counters and display cases were filled with breads, cakes, and cookies that smelled spectacular.

Mona was beaming from behind the register. Her style was evident in the warmth of the colors in the walls and the potted plants that threatened to overtake the small seating area. Mona had always wanted to own her own business and Nora couldn't think of anything she wanted to do more than take over her parents' bakery. They were a near perfect match.

Mona was a few inches shorter than Bryony, but thanks to years of sports she had far more power behind her hug. She swung her long, thick braid over her shoulder before surveying the young woman she used to babysit.

"You're too skinny," Mona said as she scrunched her nose.

It wasn't exactly surprising. The stress of graduation and finishing her senior gallery show has taken its toll on the last few months. Bryony fidgeted with the hem of her shirt before shrugging the comment off.

"The place looks great," she said, looking around

at the new pieces of art hanging on the side walls. "When did Nora's parents retire?"

"Last year," Mona sighed, though it sounded happy. "We actually just got a small contract with ACME. So, that's exciting."

The morning went by faster than Bryony thought possible in this town. The bakery was busy enough that Mona kept rising from where they were chatting to help the small groups of customers. Bryony even rose to chat when two acquaintances from high school came in for coffee.

"So, I do have an ulterior motive for visiting you," Bryony said when the breakfast rush had finally slowed.

"What?" Mona asked with mocking shock in her voice. "No way."

"My mom came in yesterday, didn't she?" Bryony tried to hide the annoyance in her voice, but knew she didn't conceal it well enough.

"She did," Mona confessed. She looked slightly guilty before ripping off a piece of croissant to pop in her mouth. "But it's not like I wouldn't have said yes anyway."

That wasn't the point. What annoyed Bryony was

that she was going to come down to ask for a job. She didn't need, or really want, her mom to do that for her. It made her feel like she was a teenager again now that she was home.

That feeling wormed its way back up to the surface and nestled into the forefront of her mind. Why had she come home, really? Did she really want to be back here? She'd asked herself this so many times since turning down her fellowship. And yet, here she was.

Bryony composed herself before asking the question anyway.

"Do you have a server position available? I'd love to apply."

Mona laughed.

"Server is generous. It's more hostess/server/busboy," she said. "I really need help in the mornings when everyone wants to order muffins and coffee and sit and chat."

"Sure, yeah, I can do that," Bryony said quickly.

Movement through the picture window behind Mona caught Bryony's eye. Someone was walking into view just over Mona's shoulder.

"Well, okay," Mona smiled. "Can you start on

Saturday?"

"Sure," Bryony said with a dreamlike quality to her voice.

The someone, who was now fully in her line of sight, had knocked the wind right out of Bryony's lungs. She hadn't turned to look at Bryony through the window, but her profile was unmistakable. Iris looked…perfect was a strong word, but it was appropriate.

Her hair was longer than the last time Bryony had seen it. It fell in brown waves just past her shoulders. Her clothes were tighter and a darker color than Iris had ever worn before, but Bryony's style had changed over the years as well. Her nose still sloped up at the tip, her lips were still thin, and her shoulders were still straight and tall. Yet there was something about these same features that seemed…off. It was as if someone had tried to create a version of her and oversharpened the edges of her image.

"Bryn?"

Mona's voice snapped Bryony back to the bakery, the table they were sitting at, their conversation. For a moment, she had been lost in a haze. Her whole body was tense, as if she was about to rise from her chair and walk after Iris.

"Oh god, sorry, I thought I just saw…" Bryony trailed off, knowing that there was no way it wasn't Iris she had just seen through the window.

Mona turned in her seat to catch the last glimpse of Iris exiting the view from the window. She didn't exactly stiffen, but when Mona turned back to face Bryony there was a tension in her body that hadn't been there before. Suddenly Mona looked incredibly uncomfortable.

"Oh, yeah. Have you, uh, seen Iris since you've been back?"

Bryony frowned.

"No, my mom said she's not staying in town so I just," Bryony paused, looking out the window again. Mona's brow furrowed. "I thought she didn't come around anymore."

"She does," Mona said simply. "Not often, but she does. She's different though."

Bryony tore her eyes from the window to look back at Mona.

"Different how?"

"Just…" Mona pursed her lips. "Just different. You're better off, trust me."

PART III

"Are you avoiding me?"

Bryony froze just before fastening the rubber band around the closed bag of coffee grounds. Apparently, Iris' voice had lost its boisterous edge while she was in Oregon. Now it was smooth and quiet like she was luring Bryony closer. It might have worked if Bryony hadn't been doing exactly what she just asked.

Bryony wasn't avoiding her because of Mona's warning or her mother's continual offhand comments. She was avoiding Iris because she had become an absolute mess since catching a glimpse of her in the bakery that morning a few weeks ago. Bryony found herself ducking into open doorways when she saw Iris walking down the street, or running into the back room to chat with Nora when she entered the bakery.

Bryony was annoyed with herself for the butterflies in her stomach, for the heat that rose up her neck and into her face, for the way her legs shook. She was also annoyed at everyone who had, apparently, lied to her when they said Iris didn't come into town often. Bryony had seen Iris almost every day since starting to work at the bakery.

It was like her sophomore year all over again. There had been a girl Bryony had never seen before that she saw one morning on her way to class. She had been standing in the lobby of the Art Conservatory building as Bryony entered, running late.

And then Bryony saw her again later that week before the same class, and again at the bodega down the block from her dorm building, and again when she was leaving the shower in her floor's bathroom. It was like once Bryony had noticed her, she saw her everywhere.

Then, just when Bryony had worked up the courage to introduce herself, after much persuasion from Amelia, the semester was over. Bryony and Amelia stayed with Amelia's parents for the winter holidays and when they got back to campus the girl was nowhere to be found.

Through that entire semester, Bryony would let her mind wander to fantasies of afternoons in cafes and museum dates. All the what ifs and could have beens that plagued her daydreams. It was a false sense of companionship that was easy to get lost in with someone she didn't know while she was incredibly lonely.

So, yes, Bryony was avoiding Iris, but it was for perfectly logical reasons.

"What would give you that idea?" Bryony asked, having mustered as much strength into her voice as she could so it wouldn't shake. "Hi, by the way."

That last bit was laced with sarcasm as Bryony turned to see Iris leaning on the counter. Her brown eyes tracked from Bryony's blue ones, down to her unsteady hands, then back up. Bryony was sure she didn't blink the entire time. Then Iris smiled.

"Hi," Iris said. She rose up to her full height. "Long time no see. Are you avoiding me?"

Bryony wanted to bite back with a "long time no text, no call, no nothing!" but she knew there was no soothing that hurt. Iris had stopped reaching out, but so had she. She had let herself give into her own insecurities of not being interesting enough once Iris left for school. She could have tried too.

The blame didn't only lay with Iris, she just didn't like to admit that. She liked to revel in the pain of it, like pressing a bruise to make sure she could still feel it. Maybe it was time to let it heal.

"Why would you care if I am?" She finally asked, turning away from Iris and stuffing the coffee in its proper cabinet. "Not that I am," she finished, quickly.

"Why wouldn't I?" Iris asked. She broke her eye contact to look over into the display case. "Are all of these fresh?"

"Yup, made this morning," Bryony said, ignoring the first question.

She walked over to the case and slipped on a pair of sanitary gloves. She needed to help Iris and get her out of here quickly. She had a feeling that Mona wouldn't be happy to see her talking to Iris. Nora was in the back so there was no risk of her hearing anything. But Bryony didn't want her to walk out here and get the wrong impression.

Iris hummed as she looked down at the pastries. She brought her hand up and tapped a finger against her lips as she looked over each baked treat.

"On second thought, I'm not hungry," Iris said. "So, why are you avoiding me?"

Instead of answering, Bryony removed the gloves and turned to grab the fresh pot of coffee.

"Can I get you some coffee then?"

Iris smiled again.

"Sure," she shrugged. "A small, please."

"Do you want room for milk?" Bryony asked.

She knew how Iris used to take her coffee, a sugar packet and some milk, but she asked all the same. Maybe her order had changed along with everything else.

"Sure," Iris said again.

Something about the way she said it made Bryony feel like it didn't matter one way or the other. It made Bryony shift uncomfortably as she poured the liquid into a small cup. She left room anyway.

"If you're so confident that you aren't avoiding me," Iris said, as Bryony rang up her coffee. "Will you meet me when you get off work today?"

Bryony pressed the "Enter" a little harder than she meant to. Yes, maybe it was time to let this bruise heal, but she hadn't meant right now. Maybe next week.

"Why?" Bryony countered this time.

The doorbell jingled and two middle aged men walked in. They stood to the side as they discussed what they wanted to order. Bryony hoped they would hurry up and decide so they could help move this disastrous conversation along.

"Because I missed you," Iris said, in a quieter voice than before.

Bryony's eye snapped back to Iris at her words and her mouth went dry. She held Iris' gaze for a few long seconds. She hadn't woken up on the edge of the woods with the green eyed woman in weeks, but she'd dreamt about her. She held it long enough to notice that the normally deep brown of her eyes was now mixed with a dark green in places. Bryony swallowed.

"Okay," Bryony said as the men started to move towards the indication markers for the start of the line. "Okay, where?"

Iris' smile grew wider.

"The reservoir," Iris said. She placed a five on the counter and picked up her coffee cup. "I'll be there all day so come by whenever. Keep the change."

Bryony fought the shiver that ran down her spine as she watched Iris exit the bakery. She didn't stop to add milk to her cup, and Bryony was sure she saw her drop it in the trash can right outside the bakery as she disappeared from beyond the window.

Iris was just as mesmerizing as she had been years ago, but Bryony was still convinced that something felt so different about the fluidity of her movements. About the way she seemed to bask in the sun as she left the artificial lights of the bakery. Something about her now made Bryony want to listen to her mom, to Mona. To stay away. Something in her mind was shouting danger.

She knew herself better than that, though. She knew she'd follow her, at least to see where it led them.

Bryony met Iris everyday after work at the reservoir. At first she was hesitant, anxiety thrumming through her as she took the well worn forest paths. They held secrets and memories that chased at Bryony's heels as she kicked up clouds of dirt.

The death that had taken room in her mom's garden had extended well into the clearing where the annual bonfire would be lit in a week. The normally lush, green vegetation was yellowing and crunched under foot when she dared to venture off the path. It sent a shiver up Bryony's spine.

Her mom's and Mona's words were still playing in the back of her head as the lapping sound of the reservoir finally grew louder through the trees. They played every time she jumped in her car to meet Iris wherever she said she'd be that day. One afternoon they'd hiked a trail into the mountains, another they'd simply laid in the grass just outside of town.

Bryony had made sure not to invite Iris to her house. She had already had a passive aggressive conversation with her mom about where she ran off to after work. Why she hadn't finished setting up her studio? Had she received a response from any of the fellowships she'd applied to? Then, of course, there was the strained look Mona gave her that morning when she asked what Bryony had planned the rest of the day.

The doubts faded away as soon as Bryony's sandled feet hit the warm sand. She saw Iris sitting on a large rock, head thrown back to soak in the sun's rays. Bryony held her breath. She was struck again by the slight differences in Iris' appearance. She couldn't describe it any way except that she looked more natural, like she belonged to the earth itself. Bryony had seen it in the green that had bled into the edges of the brown of Iris' eyes. It was in the way there were dark stains around the beds of her nails, like she'd been digging in the dirt.

Now, under the heat and glow of the sun, Iris was like a blossoming flower.

The buzz of her phone from deep inside her bag drew Bryony's attention away from Iris. She quickly swiped up on her home screen to see that the number of missed texts from Ameila had gone up. An angry red bubble with the number 10 sat in the right corner of the app. Guilt rushed over Bryony quickly, so she checked the most recent messages.

Amelia

"Well?" Iris called. Her chin was resting on her shoulder, eyes boring into Bryony's even from so far away. "You coming or what?"

Bryony smirked and shoved the phone back in her bag. She toed out of her sandals and slipped out of her clothes to reveal the bathing suit underneath.

"If you're not in the water with me in five minutes I'm dragging you in," she warned and sprinted into the calm, chilly depths.

"I'm fine here," Iris called, then gave a high shriek when Bryony sent a shower of cold droplets to litter Iris' skin.

✳

The bonfire was already in full swing when Iris met Bryony at the mouth of the forest. The bonfire itself was banned that year due to how dry the grass and surrounding plants were. The Mayor said their area was experiencing a major drought, even as they received rain on a normal basis for the season. Instead, fairy lights had been hung around the clearing and LED torches were set up to ensure the night went off without a hitch.

Bryony and Iris' hands bumped each other's as they walked the path. Their fingers were edging closer to being intertwined as they neared the sound of voices and laughter. When they reached the softly glowing lights and questioning glances, Bryony went to pull her hand away.

Iris laced her fingers more securely in Bryony's and when Bryony looked up at her questioningly, Iris gave her a reassuring smile. Not a smirk, no sarcasm or bravado behind her eyes. Bryony felt a warmth spread through her chest. She locked her own fingers and let Iris lead her into the celebration.

It didn't take long for Bryony to realize that people were talking about them. It was hard not to notice the lingering stares and the stage whispers. They'd endured it once, not that they were the first gay teens in their town. Bryony supposed that either people were surprised to see them together again or they held the same view of Iris that her mom and Mona did. After a week spent with her, Bryony didn't understand why.

Iris leaned into Bryony as they walked close to one of the tables piled high with food in everything from take-out tupperware to nice dishes. Bryony handed Iris a paper plate but noticed that she only selected a handful of finger foods for her own plate.

Bryony frowned but made no comment. She hadn't seen Iris so much as look at anything edible since that first morning in the bakery. Iris used to love food, but she also used to love coffee and was on good terms with her dad.

"Hey Bryn."

Bryony looked up to see Sean on the other side

of the table. He smiled at her and ran a hand through his, now much longer, hair.

"Hey Sean," she said and they reached over the table to give each other a swift, one armed, hug. "How've you been?"

"I've been - oh sorry," he said to the two women who were trying to maneuver around him to reach the potato salad. "I've been good. I'm home for the summer before moving to Boston."

"That's awesome," she said, taking some of the potato salad after the two women moved on.

"Yeah," he chuckled. "I'm really excited. What about you?"

"I'm home for the summer too," Bryony said. "I've been looking into fellowships in the area for the fall."

"Oh cool," Sean's voice trailed off as his eyes traveled over Bryony's shoulder. "And, uh, how have you been, Iris?"

Bryony was startled by Sean's complete shift in comfort. If there was anyone who she thought would be on good terms with Iris, it was him. Hell, he had been Iris' friend before he was hers. Bryony turned to see Iris raise an eyebrow at him.

"Fine," she said.

It almost sounded monotone, like Iris couldn't care less that Sean was there at all.

"That's…good," Sean said. He stood there for another second as Bryony tried to figure out a way to bridge the awkward interaction. "Well," he said, before she could come up with anything, "it was nice to see you, Bryn."

He beelined for a picnic table where a few other people they went to school with were already seated. One of them immediately bent over to ask him something, but he shook his head.

"What was that?" Bryony asked Iris as they walked over to a half empty line of tables.

"What was what?" Iris asked.

She swirled the liquid in her cup, but didn't drink anything.

"That," Bryony said, "with Sean. Did you guys have a falling out or something?"

"Or something," Iris shrugged.

Iris pushed the food around on her plate as Bryony ate her own. An awkward silence was radiating between them, one that hadn't been there the entire week they'd been together. It was all these people and the way they looked at Iris, at her.

Bryony looked up and saw her mom talking to two of her friends a distance over Iris' shoulder. She looked back at her plate before her mom could catch her eye and pushed at her own food a bit. After a few seconds she felt Iris' foot brush against her ankle.

"Hey," Iris said, quietly. "Can I show you something?"

Bryony raised her eyes but nothing more than that. Iris was leaning her head on her hand so her head was tilted. Her hair was falling like a curtain across her side of the table. It blocked everyone from view and for a moment everything felt peaceful again. The noise was still there, the twinkling lights, but it was just the two of them basking in their glow.

"Show me what?" Bryony asked.

"Something that will make all of this make sense," Iris said.

Her foot traveled a little higher up Bryony's leg. Bryony felt so betrayed by her own body. One week with Iris and a single touch could make her heart jump. Bryony sighed and sat up straight to look around the clearing.

Suddenly she was back in reality and that pull to

be secluded again tugged at her. It felt exactly like that feeling that pulled her home.

"Really?" Bryony hoped she sounded stern, but she was never very good at it. She crossed her arms to try and, at least, look the part. "It will explain everything? Why my mom won't talk about you? *All of this?*" She jerked her head slightly towards the lively celebration around them.

"I think so," Iris said, then paused to contemplate for a moment. "Yes," she repeated, finally. "Yes, it will."

"Okay then," Bryony said. She rose from the worn wooden bench that had surely left grooves in her bare legs. "What do you want to show me?"

The last time Iris and Bryony were in this glade was the night before Iris left for school. They laid side by side in the soft grass, and they tangled their fingers together as they stared up at the star-kissed sky. That night had been laced with a sort of sadness that neither wanted to touch. They didn't want to talk about the what ifs or the probablies. They just wanted to be. There. Together.

Tonight there was tension between them as they

laid side by side in the rough, yellowing patches. Iris' hand was laid upright between them, an offering that Bryony had yet to accept. Her own hands were clasped on her stomach as she watched the blinking of a plane's lights pass high over them.

"Bryn," Iris said. It was quiet, but so was the glade. Even the bugs seemed to have gone silent in their presence. Iris' voice sounded like it was surrounding Bryony. "Will you look at me?"

Bryony let out a heavy sigh, but made no move to turn her head.

"Will you tell me what's going on?"

"I told you I would," Iris said after a beat. "Will you look at me, please?"

"No," Bryony huffed. She stared determinedly up at the sky. "Because if I look at you I'll just want to kiss you." She crossed an ankle over the other now. "And if I kiss you I'll forget that I'm annoyed at you."

"Really? That's the trick?" Iris laughed. "All I have to do is kiss you to - " She stopped short when Bryony did not join in on her teasing. "Take my hand at least."

Bryony slapped her hand into Iris' a little harder than necessary. Iris laced their fingers together and gave them a squeeze. Her skin was so soft and warm like she had stored the rays of the sun under it for safekeeping.

Bryony swallowed. Surely a quick glance over was safe. She wanted to see Iris with her hair fanned out under her, with a smile on her wide lips. Even if it meant Bryony would give in and let Iris' beauty distract her yet again. What she saw when she turned her head made her gasp.

Iris' hair was fanned out under her, but it wasn't the dark waves that usually adorned it. Starting at her hairline, Bryony could see a staining of earth, as if Iris had rubbed soil into her roots. Her hair was laced with thin coils and small buds that mingled with the grass beneath her.

Bryony sat up to stare, open mouthed, unsure if the dark was playing tricks on her eyes. Iris' own were closed and a light smile graced her lips. The freckles across the bridge of her nose and cheeks were more pronounced against her skin, and Bryony swore she saw the beginnings of a bud peeking out of one.

"Are you - ?" Was the first thing that slipped out of Bryony's lips. "Are you still, you?"

Iris hummed, still not opening her eyes.

"I think so," she said, finally. "Most of me, anyway."

Bryony realized she should be frightened. Frightened by this being living in the skin of her past, maybe present, lover. But, she wasn't.

Not only was she not frightened, Bryony felt more at ease than she had in months. The constant pull, the questioning thoughts, they all calmed as Bryony looked at Iris.

"Can I kiss you?" Bryony asked.

Iris smiled wide now, but still, she didn't open her eyes.

"Yes," she said and without a second thought Bryony leaned in to capture her lips.

Iris smiled into the kiss and brought both hands up to rest on Bryony's cheeks. She leaned forward to catch Bryony's bottom lips between her own. Bryony moved forward with her and rested both hands in Iris' hair. She could feel the way the coils blended seamlessly into the soft strands, like they had always been there. Bryony's fingers accidentally traced over one of the buds and felt petals in its place.

She broke away from Iris, breathing deeply as Iris, finally, opened her eyes. They were green, a vibrant green that shone in the dark. Green like the eyes in her dream. Green like the grass under them.

Bryony looked down. The dying grass they had been laying on was now lush and soft under her bare legs. All around the glade the nature around them had come back to life. The trees around them had thick canopies and the flowers that should have been dormant in the dark were in full bloom.

Bryony reached out to touch one of the flowers in Iris' hair. Iris' hand caught hers and Bryony could see that same soil-like color embedded in the cuticles of her nails. It traveled up her fingers to fade at the knuckles. From there a green, like veins under her skin, traveled up her arms.

"Okay," Bryony said, watching the flower in Iris' cheek slowly open under her gaze. "You still have some explaining to do but…okay."

PART IV

The children were barefoot. Their sandals long forgotten next to their parents and their picnic blanket. Their small feet kicked up the dry dirt on the path. The pounding of their heavy steps were felt deep in the earth. Their screams of joy, their laughter reverberated off of every tree, every flower, every blade of grass.

They ran and ran until they were deeper in the woods than they had ever been before. They weaved between trees and climbed over rocks. They picked flowers and scattered their petals to lead them back home.

With each step they took, the forest felt it. With each touch of their fingers across bark and leaf, the forest felt it. With each moment they took to sit and talk, to dip their toes in the shallow creek, the forest felt it.

The shadows grew long and still the children pressed further into the woods. They should have turned back, but something pulled them forward. They did not question it. With smiles on their faces and hands clasped together, they walked further.

Hours passed but the girls did not tire. The sun went down but the girls did not fear what lay in the dark ahead of them. They were looking for something. They didn't know what but they trusted the tugging in their chest to lead them on. They trusted they would know it once they found it.

They found the heart of the forest at dawn.

The chorus of their names had been echoing through the trees for hours, but they could not hear them. They were too deep now. They were too consumed by the feeling of home.

The girls shook with excitement. They had done it. They had made it. But now they were tired.

It was almost noon when the park rangers found two girls, fast asleep under the roots of a fallen tree. They were curled close for warmth against the damp moss. Their skin was cold and their teeth chattered.

They didn't fight the men when they took them from that place, they wouldn't talk to them at all. Instead they let the rangers wrap them in blankets and carry them out of the heart of the forest. Their parents snapped the branches of bushes and crunched planets under foot as they ran to them. But no matter how many times they asked, the girls could not remember how they had gotten so lost.

The forest felt the children being taken farther and farther from them, powerless to stop it. The forest watched them go. The forest felt them leave.

PART V

Amelia

lol when you said service was bad near you I thought you were exaggerating

send me a carrier pigeon!

mine must have gotten lost navigating Brooklyn!

lmao

Kevin moved in while youre at home. Say the word and I'll kick him out for you

Missed FaceTime Call: Amelia

hey!

how's things?

Bryn?

plz send up a flare so I know youre alive

Kevin says hi! btw

Missed FaceTime Call: Amelia

miss you babe

are we good?

just wanted to make sure youre doing okay. I know stuff with you and home is always tense. if you want to move in come fall let me know cause Kevin wants to stay if not.

"Why is it all dying?" Bryony asked.

They were sitting on the banks of the reservoir. The wind blowing around them was enough to create small waves that lapped at Iris' ankles and the tips of Bryony's fingers. Her head was resting on Iris' thigh as she traced shallow shapes into the wet sand before the water washed them away.

Iris sighed. Her sandy fingers dove into Bryony's hair, massaging her scalp. She looked…normal again. Or maybe, Bryony thought, as she gazed up at Iris' face, maybe she just looked human. After all, wasn't what she saw in the woods normal now?

"Honestly, I don't know," Iris said and looked down at Bryony.

Bryony didn't avert her eyes, instead she traced

over every inch of Iris' face. She memorized where the smudged earth had stained her skin and the flowers had started to sprout from her pores.

"Can't you, I don't know," Bryony struggled to find the right words from her question, "feel it?"

"I can," Iris said, tracing her fingers down Bryony's cheek. "It hurts less when I'm with you; but that's not what you asked." She took her hand back and pressed both into the sand behind her. "I felt it when I came home after graduation and once I was home it was like I couldn't leave. Like something was keeping me here."

Iris looked up and away from Bryony's inquiring gaze. Her eyes danced over the reservoir and locked on the mangled trees that stuck up out of the deeper waters. They were once healthy, proud things that were flooded years before. Now, all that was left of them were grey, gnarled trunks that children were warned not to swim near. It meant they'd swum too far.

"I noticed that a lot of nature was beginning to die," she started again. "It was mostly in or around the woods, but as the months went on it spread. And then…" she trailed off.

Bryony rested her wet hand on Iris' shin and rubbed soothing circles into her warm skin. Iris cleared her throat.

"And then I started sleepwalking. I'd wake up at the edge of the woods, then on the path to the glade, then deep in the thick of the trees. And the further I went the more I realized that I was helping to heal the plants that were dying." She giggled and looked down at Bryony again. This time her eyes were glowing green. "I started spending all of my time there as the summer ended. I would sleep in the underbrush and watch the lichen spread along tree trunks when I touched them. I could make flowers bloom and keep the soil moist and fresh."

"What about your dad?" Bryony's voice was soft. She removed her hand from Iris' leg and began picking at the wet sand. What about her mom?

Iris' lips thinned and she turned her eyes back out over the water.

"My dad…didn't understand," she said, finally. "He tried to convince me to go back to Portland. He said I'd been better there. He said I'd outgrown this town and everyone in it."

Bryony felt like she'd been punched in the gut.

"Maybe you did," she managed to say, even if every word burned on the way out.

"No," Iris said. She sat up straighter and it prompted Bryony to sit up as well. "No, that's just it. I didn't, I thought maybe I had in college when I was meeting all these new people and in a new city but you weren't there." Iris took Bryony's hands and squeezed them. "You were missing."

"I…have a hard time believing that."

"I didn't realize it at the time, obviously," Iris said quickly. "But then I started dreaming of you in these woods. Except it was the real you, with flowers in your hair and moss in your skin." Iris was almost out of breath with how fast she was trying to get the words out. "You are all I've thought about since I came home. You are what's been missing. Since you've been back everything has been better, everything is coming back to life." When Bryony still wouldn't look at her, Iris shook her hands. "I feel complete! Can't you feel it?"

Iris' eyes were glowing green again when Bryony finally met them. She couldn't deny it, not to Iris and not to herself.

"I can," she said. "I do."

Iris was kneeling by the side of Bryony's bed, her elbows propped on the worn blankets, and a smile playing on her green tinted lips.

"Bryn," she whispered.

When Bryony didn't stir, Iris trailed soil stained fingers down her exposed arm. They left brown smudges in their wake, like she'd been working in her mom's garden. Iris leaned closer and pressed a soft kiss to Bryony's cheek.

"Bryn," she whispered into her skin. Bryony stirred under her touch. "Wake up."

"Iris?" Bryony mumbled when her eyes finally opened. "What are you - ?"

But Iris shushed her and pressed a finger to her own lips. Then she rose and beckoned Bryony to follow her with the same finger. The house was quiet, so quiet that it made the clicking of ceiling fans and the chirping of bugs outside press in around them both as they made their way down the stairs.

"Iris," Bryony whispered as she closed the front door softly behind her. Iris didn't answer. Her strides were long and purposeful as her bare feet carried her through the yard. "Iris!" Bryony's hiss was louder than she meant as she jogged to catch up.

Iris didn't stop until they were standing at the edge of the woods. It felt so familiar and Bryony was suddenly gripped by a feeling of déjà vu. Iris turned to her. Her eyes were bright in the dark, that same green that made Bryony want to lose herself in them. She smiled and cupped Bryony's cheek, angling her head so she could whisper in her ear.

"We're waiting for you."

Bryony opened her eyes. She was lying in the crater of an uprooted tree. Its exposed roots twisted above her and moss coated the ground she lay on. Bryony inhaled deeply and let the scent of the grass engulf her senses. She pressed her palms into the earth to feel it teeming with life. She smiled and stretched and for a moment, Bryony felt completely at peace.

Then, like she'd been slapped in the face, Bryony sat bolt upright. She bumped her head on one of the lower hanging roots as she scrambled to her feet and out of her makeshift bed.

"Oh my god," she choked out as her heart hammered in her chest. She bent over and put her hands on her knees as she tried to steady her breathing. "Oh my god."

"Bryn?" Iris' voice came from somewhere behind her. "Bryn, breathe," the words were closer now as Bryony felt Iris' hand on her back, rubbing soothing circles. "That's it," she said when Bryony was finally able to start controlling her racing heart, "breathe."

"Where did you take me?" Bryony asked.

Now that she wasn't panicking she could take in where she had woken up. The only word she could think of to describe it was *alive*. The earth here was untouched by people. The trees were whole and tall, the grass was long, the underbrush was allowed to roam as far as she could see.

It was like Bryony could feel it humming under her skin. She took another deep breath, her eyes closing, and let the scent consume her again. When she opened them again, Iris was watching her, studying her. A second flower was budding out of a pore at her temple.

"I didn't bring you here," Iris said, finally. "You were sleepwalking. You found me."

"But…" Bryony trailed off as she tried to remember. Surely that couldn't have been a dream. It felt so real. "But you led me here," she frowned. "You said, 'we're waiting for you.'"

"The forest led you here," Iris corrected her.

"But," Bryony looked around again. This area was so unfamiliar, so much deeper in towards the mountains than she had ever been before. There was no way she could have gotten here on her own, and especially not in the dark. "But that doesn't make any sense."

"Doesn't it?" Iris asked.

Iris walked forward and pushed Bryony's hair behind her ear. Almost mimicking the movements she had in Bryony's dream. She caught Iris' hand as it retreated and held it against her cheek.

"I don't understand."

"It wants both of us," Iris said. She rubbed her thumb along Bryony's skin, cool from the morning dew. "I've done what I can to keep everything alive but…you and me…together…"

Bryony let that sink in. Bryony crashed her lips to Iris'. The two of them. Together. She didn't really care what the cost was.

Iris smiled into the kiss, her other hand coming up to press against Bryony's other cheeks. Bryony was always taller than Iris, time and nature hadn't changed that. She let Bryony walk them backwards and press them into the trunk of a tree.

They broke apart for a moment as Bryony took a long breath. Her face was stained from Iris' fingertips, trails of soil up her cheeks and into her hair.

"Good morning," she giggled and Iris beamed at her.

"Good morning," Iris said just before Bryony pressed her mouth to hers again.

✢

"Sooooo," Mona's voice broke the silence.

It had settled around them as soon as Bryony showed up for work that morning. In truth there had been an awkwardness between them ever since Bryony started seeing Iris. Mona had never been good with confrontation and Bryony was more than happy to pretend there hadn't been an elephant in the room with them for the past three months.

"What's up?" Bryony asked.

She was loading the display case with the quiches Nora had freshly baked earlier that morning. The smell of bacon, ham, spinach, and broccoli all melded together in the prison of glass.

It was always strange going back to her job, her conversations with her mom, her childhood bedroom, after seeing Iris. She watched the condensation gather on the curve of glass from the heat of the pastries. Nothing quite seemed real after Bryony left her. It was like everything outside of her presence lacked life; like it was all a dream.

"You and Iris disappeared pretty quick the other night…"

Mona didn't look over at Bryony as she said it. Instead she kept her head bent over the bills she was counting from the register.

Bryony froze, halfway to placing the last quiche in its corner of the case. A low buzzing sounded in her ears. As if something else was moving her, Bryony turned and stared at Mona. She didn't move, didn't speak, just stared.

Mona's hands faltered for a second as she sorted through the next set of bills. Her eyes flicked briefly towards Bryony before she flipped a bill to face the rest of the stack.

Bryony frowned. She wanted Mona to continue, wanted the girl who had once coaxed her to an early bedtime while her mom worked late to question her actions. She wanted to prove her wrong. She wanted…

Bryony took a step forward and Mona finally looked up.

"Oh!" Mona shrieked.

She jumped backwards, knocking the already counted bills to the floor where they scattered towards Bryony's feet. It was as if Bryony's head broke through water. The buzzing stopped and the noises around her returned. The hum of the AC, the dripping of the coffee maker, Mona's heavy breathing.

She dropped down to help scoop up the bills, but as she did she caught a warped glimpse of herself in the aluminum lining the counter. Her eyes were a vibrant green.

"Shit!" She fell backwards and looked up at Mona.

Mona shook her head and backed up slowly. She raised her hands to keep Bryony at a distance. Bryony dropped the bills and stood.

"It's okay," she said as she tried to take a step towards Mona.

"No," Mona said, taking a step back. "It isn't."

Dawn was halfway to work when she realized

that she forgot her phone on the kitchen counter. Ordinarily, in a world before Bryony came home from school, she would have just left it there. Bryony had always been independent and she knew her work number.

Now, she reconsidered. Bryony's behavior had been worrying Dawn since before she came home. There was no logical explanation for her to just drop a fellowship and come home. Especially after she had stayed away for so long,

But she was trying to be supportive. She was trying not to pester and let her twenty-two-year-old make her own decisions. She would take a fair share of bad with the good in her life.

She pulled a U-turn and drove back towards the house. What Bryony didn't know was that Dawn had been discussing her concerns with Mona because, well, Mona had been having concerns too. Bryony had never been a snoop. She had never gone into Dawn's things growing up, that she knew of anyway. So she had no reason to believe that Bryony would unlock her phone and peruse her messages.

But Bryony wasn't Bryony these days. She was moody at home. She was distant or detached at work.

She had been spending all of her free time running around with…Iris, instead of pursuing her art. The garage sat neglected, fully cleaned but half-filled with Bryony's supplies.

Iris.

Dawn gripped the steering wheel a bit tighter as she got off the highway. She hadn't seen Iris since last fall. She hadn't come around again after Dawn turned her away.

The road back to the house was foggy and it set Dawn on edge. It had been sunny when her old hatchback left the driveway twenty minutes before. Dawn had been living with a prickle of anxiety since Bryony came home, that one day she would find Iris in her house again.

Dawn parked before the figure sitting on the front steps, fingers toying with a green leaf on an otherwise dead hydrangea bush. Apparently today was that day.

"Order up," Mona huffed and passed Bryony the large coffee and croissant.

She still wouldn't look at Bryony even though her eyes had long turned back to their natural color. There was a slice of green bleeding into the clear blue, but it was no longer shining brightly.

"Thanks," Bryony said before turning back to the line that snaked towards the door.

They didn't get many overly busy mornings. Most days Bryony could handle the rush of customers on her own. Today this influx worked to her advantage.

Mona liked to retreat to the back office during the mornings, but Nora had called for her when it became apparent that Bryony was swamped.

"Here's both of your iced teas," Mona said to the two teens through a forced smile. "Bryn will ring you up."

She almost got away as the last few stragglers cleared out an hour later. Mona was swiftly making her exit when Bryony blocked her path.

"Wait," Bryony pleaded. "Please, just, wait."

Mona's grip on the door handle tightened, but she did stop.

"What?" She sounded agitated and shifted uncomfortably under Bryony's gaze.

"Can you tell me what happened to Iris?" Bryony asked, unable to hide a hint of panic to her voice. The feeling had sat low in her stomach all morning.

"I need to know what - what happened." *What's happening,* she thought.

"Ask her yourse - "

"I did," Bryony cut her off. "But now I'm asking you." Mona finally looked at her, but quickly averted her eyes again. "Please."

"This is private property," Dawn said, closing her car door behind her.

"You used to say I was always welcome here," Iris said.

She leaned back to rest against the front door. There was no smirk on her face, no hint of smugness. She looked like the Iris that Dawn had considered as good as a daughter once.

"Things change."

Iris scowled. "I need to talk to you," she said.

As Iris did she reached for another brown, wilted leaf. It immediately began to shift between her fingers. Dawn looked away. She still didn't know what to make of that, so Dawn did what she'd done for the better part of a year. She ignored it.

"I don't have anything else to say to you," Dawn snapped and started walking towards the side door.

Dawn heard Iris' footsteps following her, across the yard and towards the door. They never sped up. Dawn gripped the strap of her bag as she ascended the rotting steps. The aged wood protested under her feet but Iris's footsteps stopped just before them.

Iris didn't ascend the steps behind Dawn as she hustled into the kitchen. She didn't move as Dawn snatched her phone from the small table and checked her messages. Nothing from Mona. Dawn couldn't decide if that was promising or not.

Iris stood like some looming presence, framed by the doorway as Dawn walked towards it. The mist was curling around Iris' ankles making it look like sunrise in November rather than a humid morning in the height of summer. Dawn didn't want to look at her. She still saw the little girl who used to help her pick strawberries, even if Iris hadn't been, well, her for some time.

"I need to talk to you," Iris repeated.

Dawn slammed the door behind her and walked on past the younger woman without so much as a glance. She heard Iris sigh and a shiver ran up her spine.

"It's Bryony, Dawn. I know you didn't want to

talk about it before, but we need to now."

Dawn felt a white hot anger crackle to life in her stomach, it scorched through her chest as it rose to her tongue. She whirled around and snarled at Iris, all neutrality forgotten.

"I told you already," Dawn spat. "You can't have my daughter. You can't do to her whatever you've done to yourself."

Years ago Dawn would have been overjoyed to see Bryony and Iris find each other again. She would have happily watched as they figured out just what they were to each other again. Not now.

"I'm not *doing* anything to her," Iris said, slowly, almost sympathetically. It made Dawn want to scream. "And it isn't up to me what she chooses next, or to you for that matter. It's up to her."

"Get off my property," Dawn hissed. "You won't see my daughter again as long as I have anything to say about it."

"It's up to her," Iris said again. "I'm sorry you can't accept that, but it's up to her."

Dawn stood there shaking as she watched Iris turn and walk towards the woods. She didn't take her eyes off of her form as it grew smaller in the distance.

Dawn did not even blink until Iris was lost in the trees. Only then did Dawn let out a desperate scream.

"When Iris got home, everything was totally normal," Mona shrugged.

She had turned the sign on the front door to "closed" before pouring herself a coffee and sitting at one of the small tables. Mona had not poured Bryony a coffee, so she did that herself and leaned against the counter to listen. Giving Mona the space she desired was working better for Bryony than cornering her had.

"She came home later in the summer though, right?" Bryony interjected. She remembered the texts from Sean that she left unread for at least a week.

"Yeah," Mona frowned, almost as if she had just remembered. "Yeah, when her dad got back from her graduation, he said she and two of her friends were moving to Portland. Then all of a sudden, in the middle of July she was home."

"No explanation?" Bryony asked.

"Well, I mean," Mona ran a finger around the rim of her mug. Bryony watched her tilt her head as she thought about her next words. "Her dad had some half-hearted excuses. Basically just said that Iris' plans fell through and she'd be home for the summer."

"Probably what my mom's been saying to people," Bryony asked, but Mona didn't answer. "I haven't seen Iris' dad all summer."

"Oh he moved, kiddo," Mona huffed before sitting back heavily in her seat. She took a long sip from her mug. "Did Iris not tell you that?"

"I never asked," she said quickly.

It was true, she hadn't asked what had happened to Iris' dad. That didn't stop her from shifting her weight a bit, passing her own mug to her other hand as she realized that Iris had deliberately worded her answer that morning around that truth.

"Yeah, he moved after the whole incident. Iris went missing for two weeks and then he moved."

"Whoa, whoa, back up," Bryony said. "There has to be more between that and..."

"Not really," Mona shrugged. "Iris was Iris for a while, a little moodier for sure, but she said she hadn't been sleeping well. Until she just disappeared."

"Yeah, okay, I get it. Everyone says she's not really Iris anymore but - "

"No, Bryn, Iris went missing," Mona cut her off.

"Like when the both of you were little. She was gone for a full two weeks and no one could find her."

"Did anyone, I mean, did her dad check that spot?" Bryony's mouth was dry, so she was impressed she managed to get the words out.

"No one could find it again," Mona said. Her eyes narrowed and her nose scrunched as if she was suddenly disgusted by something. "Too bad you weren't here, I guess. I'm sure you know where it is."

"I," Bryony tried to provide a suitable answer to the accusation. *Why would I? I can only get there when I sleepwalk? I was there just this morning? I didn't know. I didn't know!*

Mona snorted and shook her head as she turned away from Bryony.

"Wow," was all she said before she took another sip of coffee.

"I wouldn't have been able to help," Bryony finally managed.

"Somehow I doubt that," Mona said. "Anyway, you know the rest. Iris showed back up and wasn't Iris. She was freaky Iris and has been ever since. Her dad moved because he can't stand the sight of whatever is claiming to be his daughter."

"Mona, I - "

"Listen, you can go home Bryn," Mona said, curtly. "I don't need any more help today."

The coldness of Mona's voice cut deep. Bryony nodded, wordlessly before grabbing her bag from behind the counter and slowly walking to the door. She paused when she reached the door and looked at her own reflection in the glass. Her eyes were once again that bright green.

"You're wrong, you know, about Iris," Bryony said. She believed it, with her whole being. "It is still her."

"Whatever you say, Bryn," Mona sighed. "Just… just be careful, would you?"

Bryony slammed the door on her way out.

✳

"Why are you home early?" Dawn's voice broke the white noise of clicking ceiling fans and creaking floor boards.

Bryony knew that tone. It was the tone reserved for when she came home past curfew or was seen with Sean smoking behind the convenience store in town. A reprimanding tone. A mother's tone.

Dawn was sitting at the kitchen table. Her hands were folded before her and she was leaning heavily on her forearms. She looked like she might have been crying a little while ago. There was a redness to her eyes that Bryony missed as she avoided her mother's gaze.

"It was slow today," Bryony lied. She flung her bag onto the couch and stalked into the kitchen. "Why are you home?" She opened the fridge and mindlessly looked through it for nothing in particular.

"I don't want you seeing Iris anymore."

Bryony gripped the handle tightly and tried not to roll her eyes out of her head. She knew it was coming, and had felt the conversation brewing for weeks. Of course it had to bubble up today.

"Oh yeah?" Bryony asked, trying to keep her voice in check. "Why's that?"

"Because…," but Dawn trailed off for a moment. "Because I said so."

Bryony closed the fridge and turned. She was trying to keep her face as neutral as possible, not just because she didn't want to direct all of her anger at her mother, but because she didn't want to scare her the way she had scared Mona.

"Mom, with all due respect," she stopped to take a deep breath. "I live under your roof and I will follow your rules while in it, but I am twenty-two years old. If I want to see Iris, I'm going to see Iris." Bryony realized that she was digging her nails into her palm and moved her hand behind her back. "I just won't bring her here, which, out of respect for you, I haven't been doing."

"That's not good enough," Dawn said, rising from her seat. "That's not nearly good enough, Bryony. I don't want you seeing her. I don't want you becoming like her."

Bryony's phone buzzed in her back pocket. She paused to take it out and saw Amelia's name light up the screen. She silenced the call and dropped her phone on the counter top. She couldn't deal with explaining to her best friend why she had been ghosting her all summer. Not right now, anyway.

Her mother was clearly pleading with her, was possibly on the verge of tears, but she couldn't bring herself to see it from her perspective. She walked forward and hugged her. It was all she could do to make her feel better. She wouldn't like anything

Bryony had to say and she wouldn't like what Bryony was about to do.

Bryony's phone buzzed four times on the counter. Only after a long moment of her mother clinging to her like she was afraid Bryony might disappear the moment she let go, did she walk back to check the messages there.

Amelia

Well, that was that then.

PART VI

Bryony was deep in the woods.

She didn't follow Iris. She didn't follow a voice. She wasn't even sleepwalking. She didn't need to be, she knew the way now. Something in Bryony's very being was leading her as if she had taken this path a million times before.

The walk from her house in the quiet darkness was tranquil. The only noises around her were the sounds of insects and animals among the blades of grass and the groupings of shrubs. It was a white noise that rushed through her, like it was welcoming her home.

With each step she took, straying further and further from any man-made paths, a new hum of excitement shot through her. She could not only feel the forest, but all of its inhabitants and everything that made it so vast and full. She could feel Iris at the heart of it all.

Suddenly she was running. Bryony had always loved running. Her feet pounded against the forest's floor, she could feel each thump reverberate through her. Her hair whipped behind her and the smell of the foliage flooded her lungs as she tore through the trees.

Even if she closed her eyes she could find her way there, and it didn't scare her now. It didn't give her any pause or hum anxiously in her. Bryony felt free. Almost.

Iris was in the middle of the clearing. Bryony could see the way the grass around her had crawled up over her feet and up her legs. Iris looked at if she had sprouted out of the ground.

She turned when she heard Bryony enter the clearing. The grass that traveled up her limbs moved with her, the same way the soil and green traveled up the skin of her arms. Bryony could see that the flowers sprouting from her face were in full bloom now. The petals pressed into her skin.

"You came," Iris said.

There was a sliver of relief in her voice, almost as if she thought, just for a moment, that Bryony might not have.

The flowers around them were open even in the dead of night. They gave off a dull light that lit their home in an eerie glow. Bryony stepped closer until she was right in front of Iris. Her hands didn't shake as she took her hands and pressed her own thumbs into her palms. She gently rubbed at the soil there until it stained her own hands.

Iris pressed both of Bryony's hands together and held them in her own.

"Are you sure this is what you want?" Iris asked. "I know it's what I want, but you need to be sure."

Bryony looked up from their joined hands into Iris' eyes. They were less vibrant here and now but no less green. They complimented her new features well.

"Tell me what I need to do," Bryony said.

Iris smiled.

Bryony slept, in the same place she'd woken up the morning before, for seven days.

Even in her dreams, Bryony felt the roots of the trees wrap around her body. They weaved between her arms and curled tightly around her ribs. She felt the moss from its trunk creep down to cover her hair and press it deep into the earth. The grass and the ivy from the underbrush slid over her toes, her legs, up her torso until she was swaddled close to the cool touch of the earth.

Even in her dreams Bryony knew that Iris was there. She could feel her, the same way she could feel every blade of grass, every leaf, every spore of fungus. She could feel her the same way she could feel everything deep in her bones.

Sometimes Iris would lay beside Bryony, whispering to her as the days passed. Other times Iris would coax flowers to life over her body. Some large, some small but all colorful, blooming haphazardly among the maze of roots.

When Bryony woke it felt like she'd slept for years. She was waking up.

The moss that was crawling down her arms in patches bled green into her skin. The color spread to the tops of her nail beds and darkened in the creases of her knuckles. It traveled up her throat, a deep, dark green under the collar of her shirt and fading as it reached her jaw. The color seeped into her veins which stood out in her skin up to her temples and into her hair.

Her hair was like vines. They were thin and twisting with waxy leaves and large flowers in bloom. Bryony reached for a lock of vine and twisted it around her finger. The flower was an inky blue with streaks of white spidering up the petals. She brushed a fingertip over the soft petal, relishing in the warm feeling that spread through her as more flowers bloomed in her hair.

"You look…" Iris trailed off, as Bryony raised her eyes to look at her. Iris walked closer, adoration etched in every curve and angle of her face. "You're beautiful."

✳

Bryony was kneeling in her mom's garden, her hand pressed into the dry soil. On the walk back she had touched every wilted flower, every browning patch of grass, every rotting vegetable, and watched it swell with life.

Bryony watched as every plant in her mom's raised vegetable beds began to straighten. She smiled as the tomatoes regained their color and grew round. The cucumbers and zucchini were larger than she had ever seen them. The carrot stalks were bushy and vibrant.

The sound of the front door slamming open

made Bryony look up. Her mom was stumbling down the stairs towards her. Her clothing was rumpled, as if she'd slept in it or hadn't changed in at least a day or two.

Guilt gripped Bryony's chest for a moment. She'd never meant to hurt her mom, even though she knew what it would mean to walk into the woods that night. Bryony realized she should have left her a note, but she figured her mom would know where she went.

"Bryn?" Dawn asked, her voice shaking.

Bryony had caught a glimpse of herself at the reservoir before making her way here. She was able to make sure she still looked like herself, for her mom. She'd kept the ring of flowers round her head though. She liked them, liked the way they braided into her hair.

"Yeah, it's me," Bryony smiled, and for the first time in a while she felt like she really meant it. "I'm not gone, Mom." Dawn flinched at the words, and when Bryony tried to walk towards her she took a step back. "You can see me whenever you want. Whenever you're ready."

Bryony turned to leave, to head back towards the woods. Iris was waiting at the reservoir.

"Wait," Dawn's voice was small.

Bryony turned back, but Dawn hadn't moved an inch.

"Don't forget to water everything," Bryony chuckled. "I'll see you soon!"

✳

The forest welcomed them into its heart. They helped the forest grow.

A Note to our Furious Readers

From all of us at Read Furiously, we hope you enjoyed our latest installment in our One 'n Done series, *The Path Home*.

There are countless narratives in this world and we would like to share as many of them as possible with our Furious Readers.

It is with this in mind that we pledge to donate a portion of these book sales to causes that are special to Read Furiously. These causes are chosen with the intent to better the lives of others who are struggling to tell their own stories.

Reading is more than a passive activity – it is the opportunity to play an active role within our world. At Read Furiously, we wish to add an active voice to the world we all share because we believe any growth within the company is aimless if we can't also nurture positive change in our local and global communities. The causes we support are culturally and socially conscious to encourage a sense of civic responsibility associated with the act of reading. Each cause has been researched thoroughly, discussed openly, and voted upon carefully by our team of Read Furiously editors.

To find out more about who, what, why, and where Read Furiously lends its support, please visit our website at readfuriously.com/charity

Happy reading and giving, Furious Readers!

Read Often, Read Well,
Read Furiously!

More in the One 'n Done Series

What About Tuesday
Adam Wilson
978-0-9965227-9-3

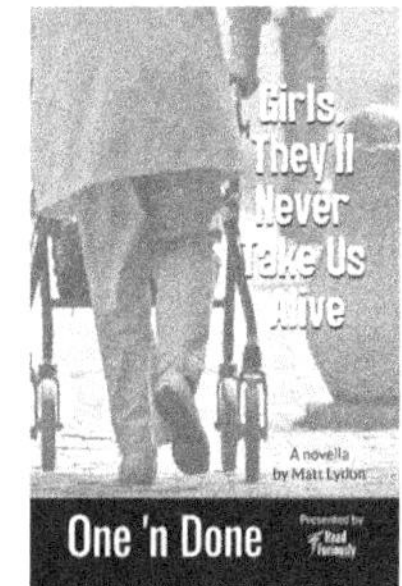

Gurls, They'll Never Take Us Alive
Matt Lydon
978-1-7337360-3-9

Brethren Hollow
Bill Hemmig
978-1-7337360-8-4

Helium
Adam Wilson
and Jeff Chin
978-1-7337360-5-3

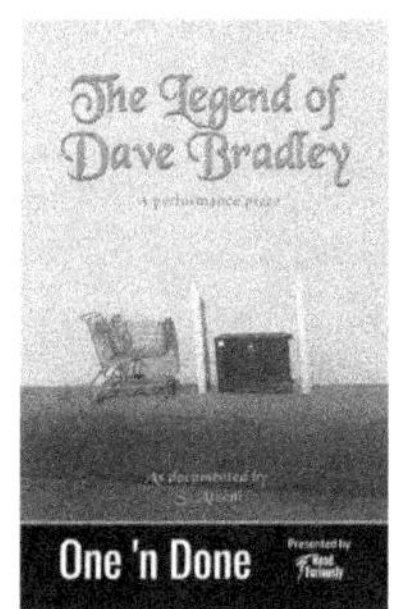

The Legend of Dave Bradley
S Atzeni
978-1-7371758-8-9

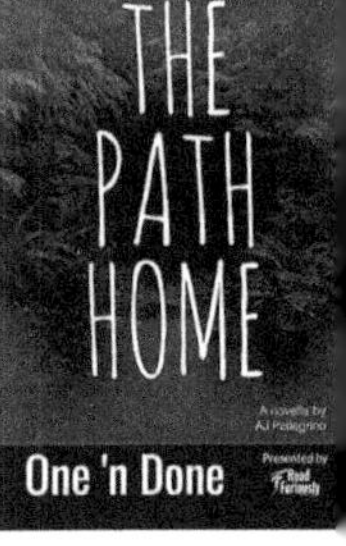

The Path Home
A.J. Pelligrino
979-8-9868097-8-6